AF230912

Squeak!

Written by Jefferson Smith

Illustrationed by Cody Cheung

Published by Creativity Hacker Press
Visit us at creativityhacker.ca

First Printing: March 2015

Printed in the United States of America

Library and Archives Canada Cataloguing in Publication

Smith, Jefferson, 1964-, author
Squeak! / Jefferson Smith.

Illustrated by Cody Cheung.
Issued in print and electronic formats.
ISBN 978-0-9919334-8-8 (pbk.).--ISBN 978-0-9919334-9-5 (epub)

I. Cheung, Cody, 1988-, illustrator II. Title.

PS8637.M5635S68 2015   jC813'.6   C2015-901386-0
                                                 C2015-901387-9

To every child who has ever squeaked alone:

Know that somewhere in this world,
there is a bright, blue box,
addressed to you, and to you alone.

What remains is to simply find it.

And therein lies adventure enough to fill a lifetime.

Now just the other day, in a
place very much like this place,
but very far away, I heard a story
about a little princess named
Brinnameade.

Princesses
were quite common where
she lived, but Brinnameade was
different. Do you know why? No, she did not have
bright green hair and a large red nose. And no, she could not
jump up and down and sing the national anthem backward.

It was
because she
could squeak. She
could squeak just like a
mouse, only louder, and she
could squeak just like a fence
gate only much prettier.

But best of all, since she only
squeaked when she was
happy, Queen Mummy and
King Daddy let her squeak
whenever she wanted.
They never told her
to shush or be
quiet.

On the particular day of this
story, though, Princess
Brinnameade was feeling
a little sad.

Would you like to know why?
No, she did not have gorillas
living in her pajama drawer.
And no, a purple leprechaun had
not stolen her favorite bicycle.

It was because she
had nobody to
squeak with.

She was an only princess,
which means she had no
brothers or sisters. And
all the other princes and
princesses were always
too busy being special
in their own castles to
come play in hers.

So with nobody to
play with, there was
nobody to squeak with
either. More than any
other thing, Princess
Brinnameade wished
that once, just one time,
when she squeaked,
somebody would
squeak back.

But that never
happened.

Until one day, after a long
and pleasant night filled with
dreams about giggling rainbows,
Princess Brinnameade woke up
and went down to the kitchen
to get breakfast.

"Good morning, Mrs. Cook," said Princess Brinnameade.

"Good morning, Princess Brinnameade," said Mrs. Cook.

"What are we having for breakfast today?"
asked Princess Brinnameade.

"We're having hot porridge and yummy toast today,"
said Mrs. Cook.

"Did you say hot porridge and
yummy toast?"
asked Princess Brinnameade.

"That's what I said," said Mrs.
Cook. "Hot porridge and
yummy toast."

"Squeak!" said
Princess Brinnameade.

She liked porridge
and toast.

Then Princess Brinnameade watched and waited to see if Mrs. Cook would squeak back, but she didn't. She was too busy setting breakfast on the table for Princess Brinnameade to eat, which she did. Yum.

After finishing everything on
her plate, Princess Brinnameade
thanked Mrs. Cook and went outside
to the garden, where she saw a tall, skinny
man kneeling in the dirt.

SEE A
DRAGON?
CALL THE
DRAGON
HOTLINE.
1-800
DRAGONS

"Good morning, Mr. Gardener,"
said Princess Brinnameade.

"Good morning, Princess Brinnameade,"
said Mr. Gardener.

"What are you planting today?"
asked Princess Brinnameade.

"Why, I'm planting big, red, ripe,
juicy tomatoes,"said Mr. Gardener.

"Did you say big, red, ripe, juicy tomatoes?"
asked Princess Brinnameade.

"I most certainly did," said
Mr. Gardener. "Big, red, ripe, juicy
tomatoes."

"Squeak!"
said Princess
Brinnameade.

She liked
tomatoes.

Then she watched, and she waited but
Mr. Gardener did not squeak back. He
was too busy moving back and forth in
the garden, pushing little tomato seeds
into the warm brown soil.

Princess Brinnameade sighed and
said goodbye to Mr. Gardener.
Then she went out to the front yard.
From there, she could see a man in
shining armor walking up the street
toward the castle.

"Good morning, Mr. Postman,"
said Princess Brinnameade.

"Good morning, Princess Brinnameade,"
said Mr. Postman.

"Do you have anything for me today?" asked
Princess Brinnameade.

"Why yes, I do," said Mr. Postman.
"I have a large, blue box with ribbons
and bows all over it,"
said Mr. Postman.
"And it is addressed to you."

"Did you say a large, blue box with
ribbons and bows all over it?"
asked Princess Brinnameade.

"Yes I did," said Mr. Postman.
"A large, blue box with ribbons and bows
all over it."

"And did you say it was addressed to me?"
asked Princess Brinnameade.

"I certainly did," said Mr. Postman.
"It is addressed to you."

Then he reached deep into his bag and pulled out a large, blue box with ribbons and bows all over it, and he gave it to Princess Brinnameade.

"Squeak! Squeak!" said the Princess. She was that excited.

In fact, she was so excited that she didn't even
wait to see if Mr. Postman would squeak back.

She took the box and ran home.

She ran past Mr. Gardener, who was
putting away his gardening tools.

She ran past the kitchen where Mrs. Cook was
cleaning up the breakfast dishes.

And she ran all the way up the stairs, into her bedroom
and slammed the door shut tight. Slam!

Princess Brinnameade had never
received a present in the mail before. In fact,
she had never received anything in the mail
before. She was so excited that she jumped up
onto the bed without taking her shoes off. First she
tore off all the ribbons and threw them over her left
shoulder. Next she tore off all the bows and threw
them over her right shoulder. Then she popped
the box open and looked inside.

It was a duck. A rubber duck. It was bright yellow and it had a big, red bill and it had a tiny, little hole in its tummy and it was perfect.

Princess Brinnameade was so happy that she grabbed the duck and hugged it tight against her chest.

"Squeak!" said Princess Brinnameade.

"Squeeeeeeak!" said the duck.

Princess Brinnameade looked down at the duck in surprise.

"What did you say?" asked Princess Brinnameade as she hugged it tight again.

"Squeeeeeeak!" said the duck.

Princess Brinnameade wasn't just happy. She was collosally, supremely, more than any birthday party ever happy.

"Squeak!" said Princess Brinnameade. "Squeak!" said the rubber duck. "Squeak, squeak!" said Princess Brinnameade. "Squeak, squeak!" said the duck.

Princess Brinnameade ran down to the kitchen.

"Look Mrs. Cook. I got a box in the mail. And in the box was a duck and the duck is yellow and it's got a hole in it and it's happy just like me!"

"Squeak!" said Princess Brinnameade.

"Squeak!" said the duck.

"Squeak!" said Mrs. Cook.

Next she ran out into the garden. "Look Mr. Gardener! I have a duck. And it is made of rubber and it has a big, red bill, and it is happy just like me!"

"Squeak!" said Princess Brinnameade.

"Squeak!" said the duck.

"Squeak!" said Mr. Gardener.

Then she ran to the gate where she could see Mr. Postman
delivering some mail to the castle across the street.

"Look Mr. Postman! That big, blue box with the ribbons
and bows all over it had a duck in it! And it can
squeak just as good as me! See?"

"Squeak!" said Princess Brinnameade.

"Squeak!" said the duck.

"Squeak!" called out Mr. Postman.

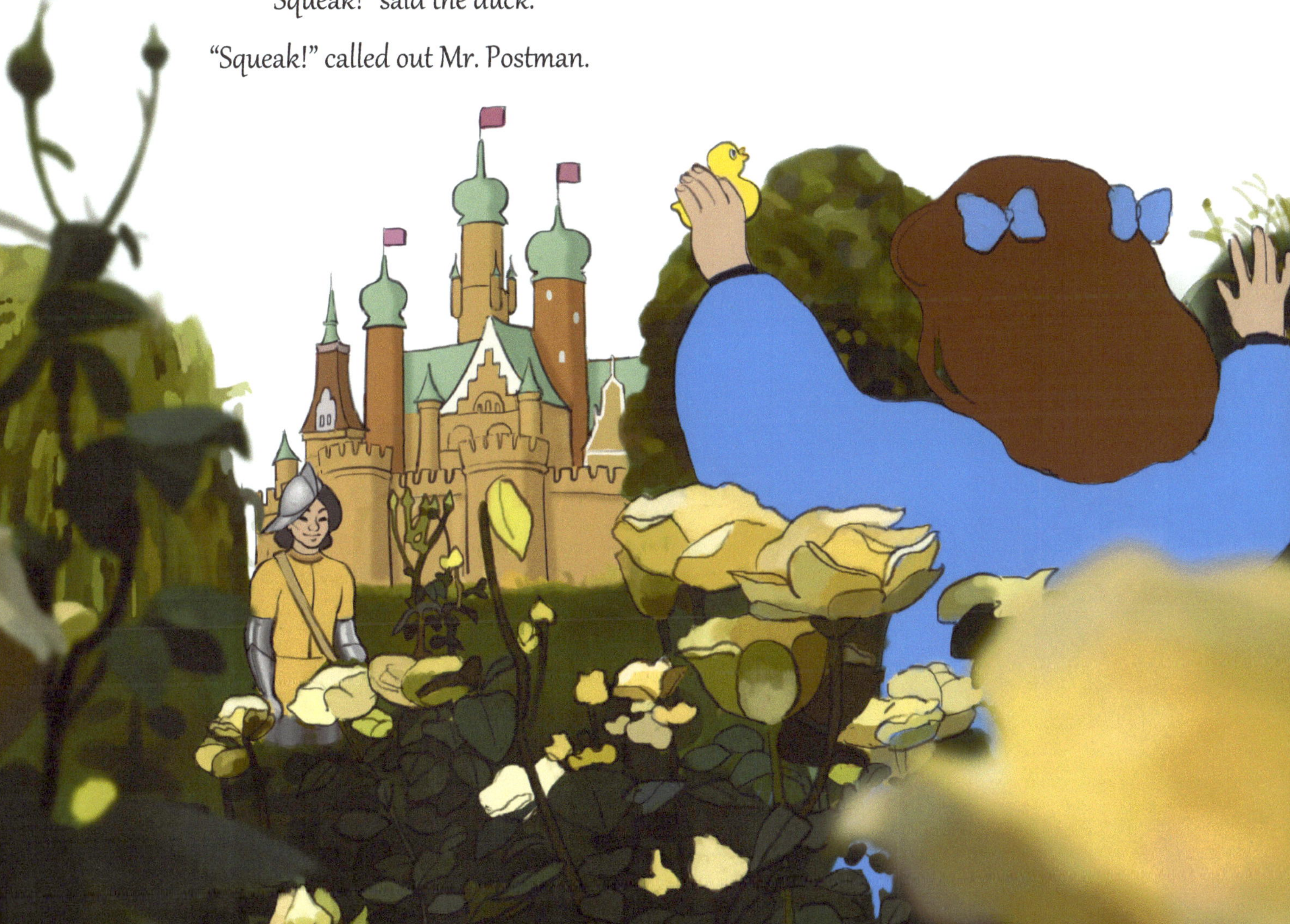

Soon everybody was laughing and squeaking.
Mrs. Cook had come out of the kitchen and was pulling Mr. Gardener
around and around the garden in a dance.

"Squeak! Squeak!" they both shouted.

Mr. Postman ran around in circles, flapping his arms like a bird.

"Squeak! Squeak!" cried his armor.

"Squeakity squeak!" replied Mr. Postman.

Then he squeaked himself across the field to join the others in their squeaky garden dance, where they all had a very good time.

And that is the story of how Princess Brinnameade finally
found a friend who could squeak right back at her whenever
either one of them was happy, which these days,
is very often indeed.

So do you know what to say if a little princess ever
comes up to you and squeaks?

EAK!

Jefferson Smith is a Canadian fantasy and science fiction writer.

Twenty years ago, while researching his first novel, he mixed up his world-jump spell and found himself in an unexpected world called Whimsy, where neighborhoods were filled with castles, rock stars worked as servants, and knights in armor delivered the mail.

In the years since then, he has told his children many times about all the wonderful things he saw there, disguising his adventures as bedtime stories, because he knew they wouldn't believe him. Especially about the rock stars.

Now that some of his children are grown up, he wanted to write down those stories to share with their children, so he made a quick world-jump back to Whimsy, to check on his facts. And it's a good thing he did, because that's when he met Cody.

Cody Cheung is now a Chinese illustrator, but she started her career as a crypto-biologist.

Five years ago, while studying leprechauns, Cody was chasing one up a rainbow when she slipped and fell off. But instead of falling back to China, she found herself in that very same world of Whimsy.

Trapped there and unable to find a way home, Cody gave up on the leprechauns and became fascinated by the people and creatures she met there. She earned her living by drawing portraits for the kings and queens who lived in all those castles, and she had a wonderful time.

But when Jefferson visited the castle where she had just finished a portrait of King Cleaner, the Dry, she decided it was time to go, and Jefferson agreed to take her back home when he left.

And so today, these two explorers of Whimsy work together in our world, telling and illustrating all the fabulous stories they heard in that strange and beautiful place.